For Nita and Frank Hilton, with love - *J.D.*
For Karen and Ken Fidgen - *F.F.*

First published in Great Britain in 1999 by
Frances Lincoln Limited, 4 Torriano Mews
Torriano Avenue, London NW5 2RZ

British Library Cataloguing in Publication Data
available on request

ISBN 0-7112-1350-X

Set in AT Administer

Printed in Hong Kong

1 3 5 7 9 8 6 4 2

THE GLASS GARDEN

JOYCE DUNBAR

ILLUSTRATED BY
FIONA FRENCH

FRANCES LINCOLN

In a city of canals and bridges, where time seemed to stand still, there lived a glassmaker, his wife and their little daughter, Lucia.

Lorenzo was the finest glassmaker in the city and had rooms in one of the Doge's palaces. This was no ordinary palace. Here, rooms opened on to gardens, gardens on to rooms, rooms on to yet more gardens.

While the glassmaker's wife sang
and embroidered silken pictures,
Lucia ran about the gardens,
chasing the coloured
butterflies and smelling
the blossoms.

One day, something terrible happened. The glassmaker's
wife was sipping fruit cordial when a bee stung her on
the lip, and she died.

The glassmaker was heartbroken. Lucia, who was too young
to understand, just thought that her mother had gone to sleep
for the winter and would wake up in the spring.

But the glassmaker was afraid for Lucia. "What if the same
thing should happen to my daughter?" he said. "Then I would
have no one left in the world to call my own." He decided to
move to a rocky island just across the lagoon, where nothing
would grow. There were no birds to sing, but no bees to sting
either, so his daughter would be safe.

He set up his glassmaking furnace and once more began to make glass. He made goblets and wine glasses, beakers and bowls so exquisite that princes all over the land wanted to buy them.

But Lucia began to pine. Not only was she without her mother, there was no garden to play in. She sat in silence, watching her father at his work.

"I'll make something specially for you," he said one day, and he presented her with a beautiful glass lily. Lucia smiled. So the glassmaker made whole clusters of lilies, in purple, white and gold. Lucia seemed happy again.

Over the weeks and months, the glassmaker made a glass garden. There were poppies and orchids, apple and peach blossom, passion flowers, pomegranates and prickly pears. There was morning glory climbing up to the balcony and angel's trumpets that tinkled in the wind.

But although Lucia smiled more often, she never danced or played. The glassmaker asked her why.

"The glass garden is beautiful, father, but there are no butterflies."

So the glassmaker made multicoloured butterflies that perched daintily on the flowers as if poised in mid-flight.

But Lucia was still melancholy. Again, the glassmaker
asked her why.

"The glass butterflies are beautiful father, but there are
no birds."

So the glassmaker made glass birds that seemed to fly
through the glass fountains.

But Lucia was still melancholy, and once more her father
asked her why.

"The glass birds are beautiful, father, but there is no scent."

The glassmaker gave a deep sigh. He knew that a perfumed
garden would attract bees, and this he dared not chance.

So, on the edge of a city where time seemed to stand still,
Lucia lived in a garden where time stood even stiller. There
was no spring, no summer, no autumn, no winter. The flowers
were always in bloom.

But time did not stand still for Lucia. She grew up into a beautiful young woman; she too was in bloom. She moved wistfully amongst the delicate flowers of the glass garden, taking care not to break them.

Every year at carnival time, Lucia listened to the music and watched the fireworks high above the city, great chrysanthemums of light exploding and filling the sky one minute, vanishing the next.

How she longed to go to the carnival, to wear a mask like all the other revellers, to dance and sing in the streets! But her father would not hear of it.

"The city is full of dangers," he told her, "plagues and pestilence, cutpurses and vagabonds. You are better off here with me."

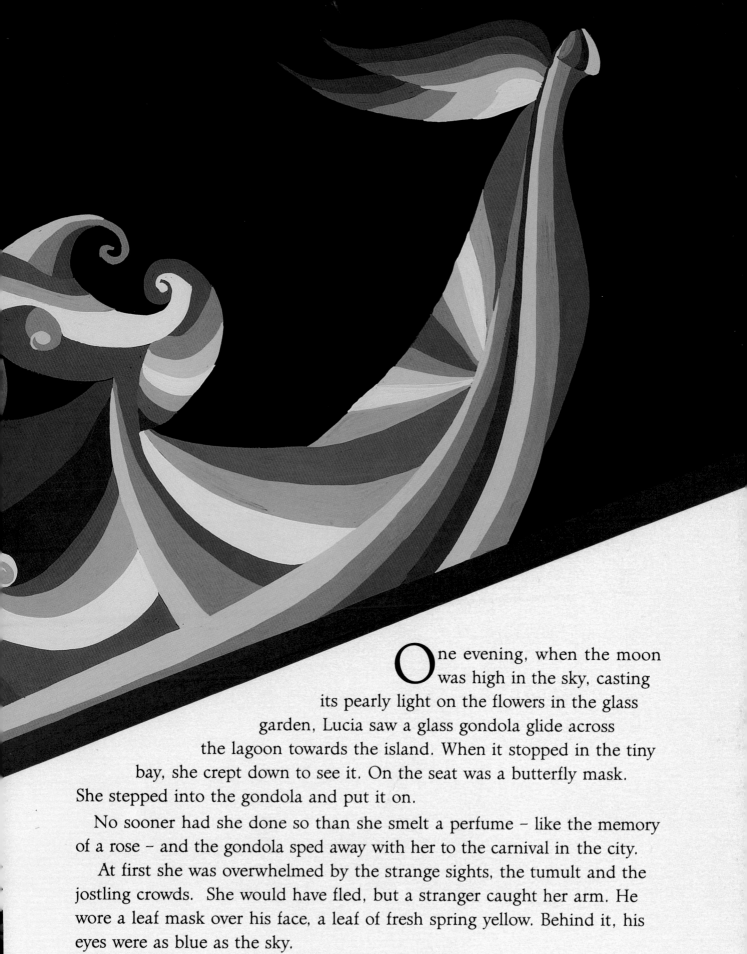

One evening, when the moon was high in the sky, casting its pearly light on the flowers in the glass garden, Lucia saw a glass gondola glide across the lagoon towards the island. When it stopped in the tiny bay, she crept down to see it. On the seat was a butterfly mask. She stepped into the gondola and put it on.

No sooner had she done so than she smelt a perfume – like the memory of a rose – and the gondola sped away with her to the carnival in the city.

At first she was overwhelmed by the strange sights, the tumult and the jostling crowds. She would have fled, but a stranger caught her arm. He wore a leaf mask over his face, a leaf of fresh spring yellow. Behind it, his eyes were as blue as the sky.

Lucia danced the whole night long with the stranger –
but before the morning came and her father could
discover her absence, she sped home in the glass gondola.

On the second night, it took her to the carnival again,
only this time she wore the bird mask she found waiting.

The stranger wore a mask of brilliant summer green.
Behind it, his eyes were as green as the lagoon.

On the third night, Lucia went yet again. This time she
found a moth mask in the gondola. The stranger wore a
leaf mask of burning gold. Behind it, his eyes were as
brown as the earth.

"Tonight the carnival ends," the stranger said to Lucia. "Take this as a parting gift." And he gave her a sweetly-scented rose tree in a pot.

Lucia sighed. It was the same perfume that she had smelt each time she put on a mask. "I cannot take this to the island," she said. "My father won't allow real flowers."

"Take it," said the stranger. "Although it smells so sweetly, the rose is made of glass."

So Lucia took the rose home and placed it in the garden beside the fountain. She began to stroke the petals, when out of it crawled ... a glass bee!

Lucia could not remember seeing a bee before. When she picked it up between her fingers, she felt the sharpest sting.

But Lucia did not die. In the glass garden, stung by a glass bee from the glass rose, Lucia turned into glass.

How her father grieved! How bitterly he wept! "What was the use of all my care," he lamented, "if my daughter too has turned to glass?"

And he no longer tended the glass garden, so that spiders came and span silken cobwebs, from stalk to flower to leaf. By moonlight, the garden seemed caged in nets of silver; by sunlight, in nets of gold.

Lorenzo sent far and wide for physicians to bring his daughter back to life. None succeeded – but his appeals reached the ears of the stranger.